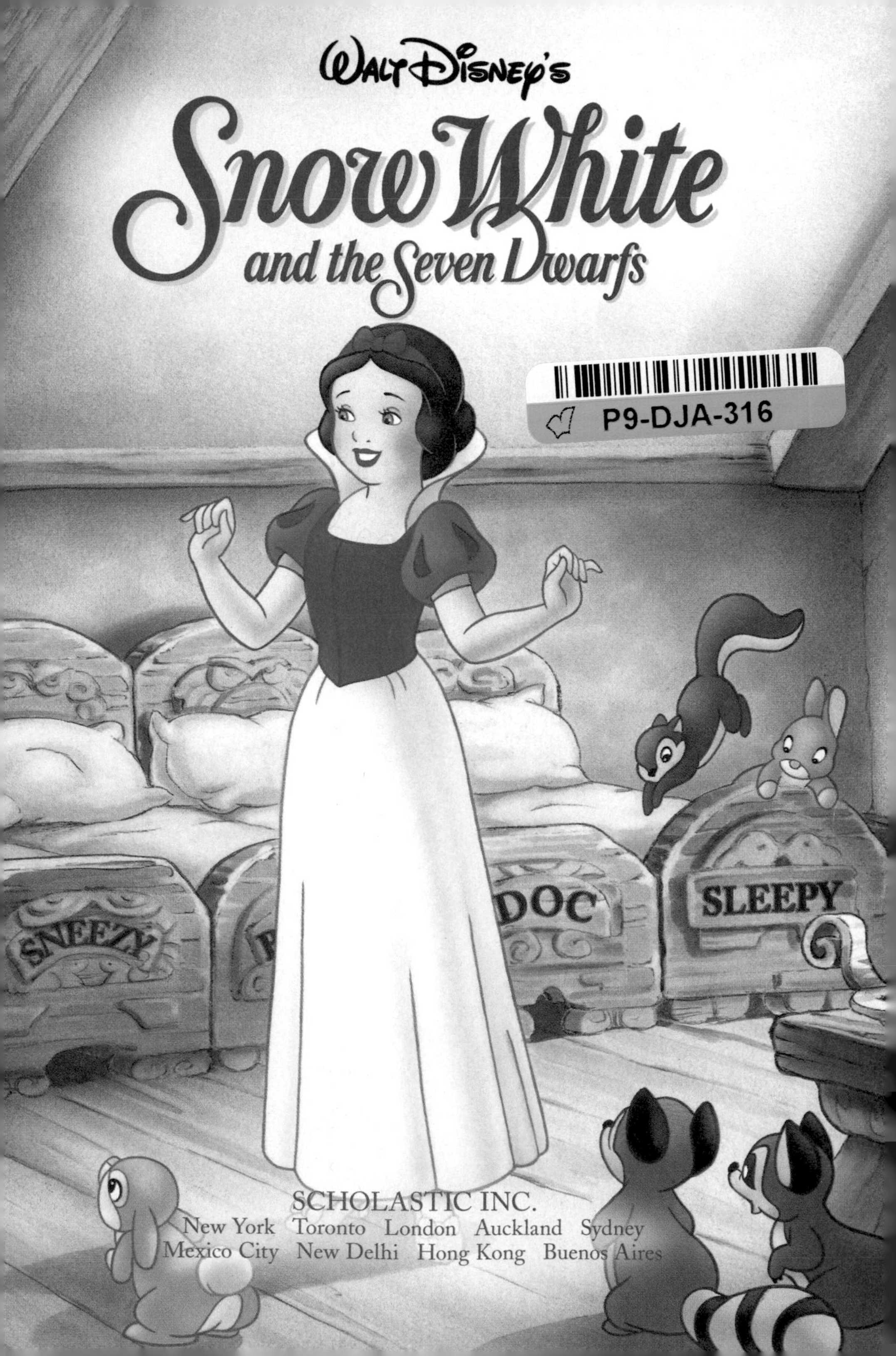
Walt Disney's
Snow White
and the Seven Dwarfs
P9-DJA-316
SNEEZY
DOC
SLEEPY
SCHOLASTIC INC.
New York Toronto London Auckland Sydney
Mexico City New Delhi Hong Kong Buenos Aires

Once upon a time, in a faraway castle, a little princess was born. Her parents named her Snow White.

As the years passed, the child grew into a lovely young woman. Her beauty and her gentle nature won the hearts of all who knew her.

After her father died, Snow White lived in the castle with her stepmother, the Queen.

The Queen was very beautiful, but she was cold and heartless. She was also jealous of Snow White's beauty. So the Queen dressed the Princess in rags and forced her to work as a maid.

The Queen's most prized possession was a magic mirror. She would stand in front of the mirror every day and ask, "Magic Mirror on the wall. Who is the fairest one of all?"

And every day the mirror would reply, "You, O Queen, are the fairest in the land."

Meanwhile, Snow White worked long hours in the castle. She always did her chores with a smile, often singing while she worked.

One day, as she drew water from the well, she sang a song about her fondest dream. She wished a handsome prince would come to the castle and carry her away.

"Please make my wish come true," whispered Snow White, looking into the well.

No sooner had she said these words than a handsome prince appeared next to her.

The Prince fell in love instantly, but Snow White was shy and fled to the castle.

That evening, as usual, the Queen asked the mirror, “Magic Mirror on the wall. Who is the fairest one of all?”

But this time her mirror replied, “Lips red as the rose, hair black as ebony, skin white as snow.”

"Snow White," the Queen exclaimed. The Queen was so furious that she immediately called for her huntsman.

"Tomorrow, take Snow White far into the forest and kill her," she commanded.

Then the Queen gave the Huntsman a jeweled box and told him to bring her proof that he had obeyed the order.

The Huntsman agreed.

The next morning, the Huntsman took Snow White deep into the forest. He watched as she picked flowers. At that moment the Huntsman knew he could never harm this kind girl.

“My dear Princess,” the Huntsman said, “you are not safe. The Queen is jealous. She has ordered me to kill you, but I could never hurt you. Run into the forest and never return!”

Frightened by his words, Snow White did as she was told. She ran and ran until she could run no farther.

Lost and alone, Snow White sank to the ground and sobbed herself to sleep.

The Huntsman placed an animal's heart inside the box the Queen had given him and presented it to her that night. The Queen rejoiced, for she believed the Huntsman had carried out her order.

"Now I am the fairest one of all!" she exclaimed triumphantly.

When Snow White awoke the next morning, she found herself surrounded by forest animals.

Curious birds, rabbits, squirrels, chipmunks, and even a mother deer and her fawn crept up for a closer look.

Snow White smiled. She didn't feel lonely any longer!

"Do you know of a place where I can stay?" Snow White asked her woodland friends.

In response, two birds chirped and began to tug gently at her cape. So she followed her new friends to a tiny cottage nestled among the trees.

"Oh! It's just like a doll's house!" Snow White said.

Snow White looked inside the cottage.

"Oh, my! What a terrible mess!" she cried. She stared in wonder at the seven little chairs. "Seven children must live here," she said. "I'll just tidy up a bit and surprise them. Perhaps they'll let me stay for a while."

Snow White began to clean the cottage. The animals helped.

Snow White went upstairs, where she found seven little beds lined up in row. Each one had a name carved on it.

"Happy, Dopey, Grumpy, Sneezy, Bashful, Doc, and Sleepy," she read. "I'm a little sleepy myself," she added, yawning. Snow White lay across the tiny beds and promptly fell asleep.

Meanwhile, seven little men were hurrying home from a hard day's work in the diamond mine. They didn't know it, but they had a surprise waiting for them. For these were the Seven Dwarfs who lived in the cottage where Snow White was sleeping.

They sang merrily as they walked through the forest. Doc led the way with the lantern. Behind him were Grumpy, Happy, Sleepy, Bashful, Sneezy, and, last of all, Dopey.

As the Dwarfs entered their cottage, they noticed things were different. Everything was neat and tidy!

"Someone's been here!" cried Doc.

"M-m-maybe it's a goblin," said Bashful. "And m-m-maybe it's still here!"

"Only one way to find out," said Grumpy.

So up the stairs they went.

But instead of a goblin, the Dwarfs found Snow White, fast asleep on their beds.

"It's a girl!" declared Doc.

"She's beautiful," added Happy.

Snow White was awakened by their voices.

"Why, you're not children at all," she said, surprised. "You're little men."

"That's right," said Doc. "But who are you?"

Snow White introduced herself and told them all about the wicked queen.

“You can stay with us,” said Doc. “We won’t let anything happen to you.”

All the rest of the Dwarfs agreed.

Back at the castle, the Queen once again consulted the Magic Mirror. This time, the mirror said, “Over the seven jeweled hills, beyond the seventh fall, in the cottage of the Seven Dwarfs, dwells Snow White, fairest one of all.”

The Queen was outraged. “The Huntsman lied!” she shouted. “Now I will have to take care of her myself!”

The Queen ran to a dungeon room. She quickly mixed herself a magic potion.

After she drank the potion, the Queen instantly turned into an old woman.

Then she cast a magic spell over a luscious red apple. "One taste of the poisoned apple and Snow White will sleep forever!" she cackled with glee.

That night at the cottage, Snow White cooked a special meal for the Dwarfs.

“Supper’s almost ready,” she told them. “You’ll just have time to wash.”

“Wash?” asked the Dwarfs.

But Snow White was firm. So they all went outside to scrub themselves clean. Even Grumpy got a soaking!

After dinner, it was time for some fun! The Dwarfs played their musical instruments and took turns dancing with Snow White.

Dopey climbed onto Sneezy's shoulders and covered them both with a long coat. Now he was as tall as Snow White—but not for long. One sneeze from Sneezy sent them both tumbling to the floor.

Before they set off for work the next morning, Snow White gave each Dwarf a good-bye kiss.

"Beware of strangers," warned Doc. "No telling what that wicked queen might do."

"Don't worry," replied Snow White. "I'll be careful."

After the Dwarfs left, Snow White began making pies. Soon after, an old woman appeared at the window.

"All alone, my pet?" the old woman asked. "How would you like to taste one of my nice apples? They're wishing apples, you know," she added.

The animals recognized the Queen at once, but Snow White did not.

"They do look good," Snow White said.

Snow White took the apple and made a wish.

As soon as she bit into the apple, she fell to the floor.

Only love's first kiss could wake the sleeping princess.

"Ha, ha, ha!" cackled the Queen.

The animals hurried to the diamond mine to inform the Seven Dwarfs that something was wrong.

The animals tugged at the Dwarfs' clothes until the men understood that something bad had happened. The Dwarfs jumped onto the deer and headed for the cottage.

On their way, they spotted the old woman—and recognized the Queen in her disguise!

"Follow her!" Grumpy shouted. So the Dwarfs chased her all the way up a steep cliff. The Queen was trapped!

Suddenly a bolt of lightning struck the cliff. With a horrible scream, the Queen fell to the jagged rocks below. The wicked Queen was gone forever!

When the Dwarfs finally arrived home, they found Snow White asleep on the floor. Nothing they did could wake her.

With tears in their eyes, they gently laid Snow White on a bed.

The next day, the Dwarfs built a crystal casket for Snow White. Then they carried it to a peaceful glen in the depths of the forest.

For many days, the Dwarfs stayed by Snow White's side, hoping she would wake up. But Snow White slept on and on.

Meanwhile, the lonely prince had been searching far and wide for Snow White. One day, he heard about a beautiful maiden who slept in a crystal casket in the forest, surrounded by seven little men.

Finally, he came upon Snow White. "At last I have found you," the Prince whispered. Then he kissed the sleeping princess.

Snow White opened her eyes. The spell was broken!

The Prince gathered Snow White in his arms and lifted her onto his horse. This time, Snow White was not afraid of her handsome prince.

"Good-bye!" she called out to the Dwarfs. "You have been good, kind friends. I will never forget you."

Snow White kept her promise. She included the Dwarfs in all the festivities at the castle, where she and her prince married and lived happily ever after.

The End

Eye Spy

Hi, ho, hi, ho! It's back to the story you go! Try to find these pictures in the story.

This Royal Book
Belongs to
Beatriz

 Published by Scholastic Inc., 90 Old Sherman Turnpike, Danbury, Connecticut 06816.

For information regarding permission, write to:
Disney Licensed Publishing,
114 Fifth Avenue, New York, New York 10011.

ISBN: 0-7172-8343-7
Printed in the U.S.A. First printing, January 2007